I0788203

TODAY WAS TOMORROW YESTERDAY

Everything Can Change Instantly, So Follow The Sun

BY

Sal LeDonne

Copyright © 2025 Sal LeDonne

All rights reserved. No part of this publication may be reproduced, distributed, or transmitted in any form or by any means, including photocopying, recording, or other electronic or mechanical methods, without the prior written permission of the author, except in the case of brief quotations embodied in critical reviews and certain other non-commercial uses permitted by copyright law.

ISBN:
978-1-965936-75-7
LCCN:
2025912398

Dedication

This book is joyfully dedicated to my loving family, for whom none of this would have been worth it without them. I also keep in my heart the family members who have passed before me, especially my grandparents who immigrated from Italy.

About the Author

Sal LeDonne has been a writer for most of his life. He's published many articles and poems, and now comes his first novel, "Today Was Tomorrow Yesterday."

His book of poetry, "Seasons of Life and Love," came out in 2003 and was received well for Sal's creative spirit.

Retired now, he has more time for his writing ideas to come to life.

Sal was a professional landscape designer for over 40 years. He owned and managed both a laundromat and a car wash. He's been active in many sports and is a Eucharistic minister at two Catholic parishes. He holds an associate's degree in Business Administration and Horticulture from Morris County College in New Jersey.

Mr. LeDonne is a devoted family man who enjoys the simple pleasures of life. In his free time, he finds joy in watching classic old movies, browsing garage sales, and spending quality time with loved ones. His hobbies include playing guitar, golfing, gardening, and bowling. A passionate collector, he especially enjoys gathering baseball cards and unique memorabilia.

He is happily married to his lovely wife, Patricia. Together, they have raised four grown children and are now looking forward to welcoming grandchildren into their lives.

Table of Contents

Preface

It is a broken society, years after the catastrophic events took place. Slowly, the societal differences are revealed to the reader. Little by little, how people are actually living and behaving in their day-to-day life.

There are no cars or planes, only buses and trains for transportation. The state has implemented many new restrictions. Most books are banned (that contain original thought and opinions). All media is controlled by the state and enforced by the Marshall Law Military Police. Nearly everyone carries a backpack with all essentials needed, food, water, or almost anything desired, as long as it fits inside. It is provided free by the state. All work is done on a "voluntary" basis to help all state-run activities. Any dissent is strictly forbidden and immediately enforced by the Military Police.

The main characters in the story – Jake, Emily, and Jerry – "volunteer" at the "Renewal Road" cleaning up and rebuilding after each "riot" that destroys the fake neighborhood. The state will treat citizens for medical needs for free as long as you are deemed "repairable." It's a bleak and nearly hopeless way of life. As we get to know our characters, they usually meet and talk during breaks at the picnic area by the nearby lake. People and children are always seen wandering around the area. People just want to understand the activity and behavior that takes place on a daily basis on "Renewal Road."

Is there hope that's just around the corner? Today Was Tomorrow. Yesterday is a heartfelt journey through grief, hope, and quiet rebellion in a world where rebuilding isn't just about bricks and mortar—it's about healing the human spirit.

Chapter 1
Religion or Garbage Day?

It was Friday.

The streets still glistened from last night's drizzle, a gray sheen coating the concrete like old sorrow. The bus stop was busier than usual. Some people clustered in small groups, exchanging murmured words. Others clutched Styrofoam and paper cups, sipping bitter warmth. A few just stood there—silent, staring—not at anything in particular, but into the kind of distance that speaks of weariness too deep for words.

A young woman approached the bench. A child rested against her hip, his small arms clinging to her. In her other hand, she dragged a torn plastic bag, heavy and swollen with what looked like trash, but felt like so much more.

She lowered herself onto the bench slowly, bone-tired. The bag thudded between her feet. Her face was drawn; her arms and back strained with a quiet ache. Her hands, red and raw, looked like they had been at work far longer than the morning should have allowed. When the child fussed, she instinctively tucked a pacifier into his mouth. He calmed. She did not.

Her pants sagged from her hips, loose and unkempt. Her chest rose and fell in tired, uneven rhythms. Breathing itself seemed a labor.

From the corner, a garbage truck roared up and screeched to a halt. One of the workers—bearded, in a worn city-issued vest—hopped off and began hauling bags left along the curb. He worked efficiently, but his eyes kept drifting toward the crowd at the bus stop.

Not far off, a man stood with a tagboard sign strapped to his chest. The usual slogans—faith, salvation, doom, redemption. Most passed him by without a glance. But one man, older, weathered, dragging a lumpy canvas sack behind him, stepped toward the truck.

The old man made eye contact with the garbage collector.

"I'm going to call my son this morning," he muttered. "Haven't spoken to that boy in nine years."

"That's good, Mr... —"

"Johnson," the old man said, wiping his hands on his coat. "Trying to get rid of the old habits. That's the real load."

The bearded collector gave a knowing smile and hefted the old man's bag into the truck. He pulled a lever, and the motor howled as the contents were crushed beneath industrial teeth.

"Anyone else today?" he called out toward the crowd at the stop.

Most turned away. A few looked down—ashamed, uncertain, maybe even tempted, staring at their own sacks resting by their ankles.

"Chris! You done?" a voice barked from the truck cab. "Come on—we're behind schedule!"

"Just a sec!" the collector yelled back.

Chris took a few steps closer to the crowd, his voice gentler now. Encouraging. Familiar.

It was garbage day.

And then—he was gone.

Same thought. Darius stared at the wet pavement as if it might give him answers.

The woman with the shawl still damp from the drizzle blinked in disbelief and sipped her latte. The warmth didn't reach her hands.

"How 'bout you, buddy?" Chris asked a wiry young man clutching a shiny duffel bag.

"Okay, Lee," the young man muttered. "Have it your way. I'll see you next garbage day."

He turned away, but something had changed in his face. Something lighter, like maybe he'd finally exhaled after a long time.

He walked toward the woman on the bench and met her gaze. No judgment. Just quiet understanding.

He knelt before her, slipped off a glove, and reached up to wipe a tear from her cheek with his thumb. It wasn't a romantic gesture. It was sacred. Gentle. True.

"You don't want to carry that anymore, do you?"

She looked down at the bag.

It had been years since she allowed herself to really look at it. At what it held. At what she had dragged with her, stop to stop, through life.

"Chris! Let's go!" the driver barked again, growing impatient.

The old man shuffled past once more.

"I'm going to go home and call my son this morning," he said again, this time with a little more conviction.

A man in a worn suit, puffing on a half-lit cigar, called out, "Yeah, you do that, old-timer. Long time coming."

At the back of the truck, a slow drip began to fall from the compactor. A viscous stream slid down and splashed onto the asphalt.

Was it raining? Or something else?

A tear from the old man's bag, maybe.

Chris turned to the woman one last time.

"It's Wednesday. And Friday. That's when we take away all your garbage so you can have a clean slate, mam."

A man nearby flicked his half-lit cigar into a puddle

She nodded, barely. Of course. Everybody knows that.

But still—how do you hand it off? How do you give away what you've grown used to carrying? Even if it breaks your back. Everyone's got their own burdens. Who wants another?

Not today, she thought. Not this Friday. Chris leapt onto the back of the truck and grabbed the side rail.

"Let's roll!"

Steam hissed into the morning air as the truck rumbled forward, its engine humming like a hymn.

Around the bus stop, the conversation began again softly. A few puffs of a cigar. A few sips of latte. The baby's pacifier popped gently back into place.

The bus arrived on time, doors hissing open. People gathered their things—some slung their burdens back over sore shoulders. Others dragged them behind, stepping up onto the bus one by one.

She stayed on the bench.

Still.

A whisper to herself, just a moment ago:

"I'm sorry."

Her eyes lowered to the bag for the second time in years.

And this time—

She called out, but what else can I do?

Sometimes you are just not ready to part with whatever has been bothering you.

Not today anyway.

Not this Friday.

Chapter 2
Jerry and The Sun

Once the garbage truck pulled away, I began walking down the block. Many of the buildings in this neighborhood were in ruins—just piles of rubble were poured out onto the sidewalks. I saw the post office up ahead and figured I'd check my mail.

As I entered the post office, I grabbed my keys from my coat pocket and felt for the right key to Box #7432. When I found it, I opened the box. The usual stack of envelopes stared back at me as I sifted through the mail.

A thought briefly crossed my mind—something fleeting and uncatchable. I closed the box, turned around, and started heading for the exit.

That's when he stopped me.

"Where the hell are you headed, friend?" he asked.

His voice was rough around the edges, but not unkind.

I paused. His directness caught me off guard.

"Just running errands," I replied.

There was something in his eyes—an exhaustion deeper than sleep could fix. I couldn't help but feel a pang of sympathy. Life had clearly not been gentle with him. He looked like someone who'd been through twelve rounds and was still standing.

"I'm taking the bus out to Renewal," I said.

"Wanna come to lend a hand? I'm sort of a—"

"Shift supervisor there. I'll get you something to do out there. Come and help out."

"Thanks," he said.

"Glad to help out."

His words lingered longer than I expected. There was something disarming about the way he spoke—not just what he said, but how he said it. No fanfare, no pretense. Just an open hand. An invitation.

That was my first encounter with Jerry.

"We can take the next bus out," I said, offering a hand.

"I'm Jake."

"Jerry," he nodded.

I shook his hand, and Jerry got his stuff together and put several items in his backpack. I remember asking him what his book was. He told me it was the Holy Bible. He was reading it. I held off on a comment about the book. I knew it was on the banned list, but Jerry wasn't bothering anybody.

I felt we headed out the door together and went down to the bus stop to wait for the next ride. Ten or twelve others were waiting as we approached.

I commented to Jerry that it was turning into a nice day.

He smiled and only added, "It's always nice with the sun."

And I agreed.

Chapter 3
Emily and the Stars

We boarded the bus and made our way down the aisle, weaving past seated passengers until we spotted an open seat toward the back. There was no rush. The bus moved along steadily, and the hum of the road outside felt almost calming. I picked a seat on the left side and eased into it, letting myself settle. After placing my backpack on the seat beside me, I leaned against the window and looked out.

Minutes passed quietly. I felt a presence beside me—a young woman had stepped into the aisle. She looked at me, smiled politely, and asked if she could sit next to me. Without hesitation, I moved my backpack to make room. She slid in gracefully.

There was something soft in her demeanor—an unspoken kindness that lingered behind her smile. Her beauty was subtle but undeniable. She didn't wear it loudly; instead, it lived in her expressions, in the quiet confidence with which she sat. Her coyness wasn't performative—it was simply there, gentle, natural. But beneath her calm exterior, I sensed a kind of heaviness, like her face still carried traces of rain it had once weathered.

She sat on my left, with her belongings tucked neatly on her lap. I noticed bundles of coins gathered in her left hand, and in her other hand, she held an open container of Chinese food and two shop sticks, an unusual but oddly charming combination. I found myself impressed by her simplicity and her self-sufficiency.

That's when I first spoke to Emily.

Emily looked up at the sky through the bus window, then turned to me.

"Don't you think the stars are staring at us?" she asked.

I smiled and said, "Do you think they're stars up there?"

"What do you mean?" she said, her voice carrying both curiosity and challenge.

"If they're not stars," I said, "maybe they're something else."

She tilted her head slightly.

"Like what?"

I shrugged.

"Oh, I don't know... like lights from a box. Maybe someone or something out there is watching us."

Her eyes lit up, and she grinned.

"Well, what if that's how we breathe?" she said.

"What if the sky poked holes in the box just so we could breathe?"

I paused, stunned by the image.

"Wait, what?"

Was she serious? Was this her sense of humor? Or was she simply… different? I couldn't tell. But something about her made me want to keep listening.

She leaned back, her smile fading just a bit.

"I came from a broken home," she said.

"No father. A lot of empty promises. No real structure. No family."

Her words landed heavy, but they weren't meant to draw pity. She wasn't looking for that. It was just her truth, laid bare.

"I wish this dream was real, I could go to the supermarket, buy a few cans of love, and put them in my shopping cart... and a large box of family, so I could finally be happy." There was a pause.

"It just doesn't work that way," I added.

The words stung with their own truth.

By the time we arrived at the Boston Central Port Authority, something between us had shifted. Neither of us said it aloud, but we both felt it—we didn't want to part ways.

Instead of going in separate directions, we chose to stay together.

Emily. Jerry. And me.

We agreed to take the next bus together, departing at approximately 5:15 p.m.

And just like that, three strangers became something more.

Chapter 4
Jake and His Dad

Jake took a nap on the bus.

He remembered when he was a little boy, about 8 or 9, and would go to work with his father. He always thought it was funny how everyone knew his father wherever he went.

"What's up, Jake's Dad !?"

"Boy, you always take your kids to work, huh, Joseph?"

Jake's father, Joseph, rarely remembered names, who it was, always: "Hey thanks kiddo" or "How you been kiddo, what's going on on your end?"

Jake would watch and learn during those summer vacations. He'd watch Dad drive the truck to the job sites where they were building new houses. And he was so proud of his father's work and the job that he did.

His father, Jake, would think to himself that he must be the richest man in the world because his work was so important—surely they couldn't build all these houses and stores without him. And he seemed to have millions of friends. Everybody knew

Joe, and that made Jake thrilled. All day, riding on that truck with his dad.

It was about that time in Jake's life that he discovered his "Special Gift." A secret he kept to himself. He had told his mom and dad about it when it happened. So he never felt guilty for keeping it a secret from others.

The first time it happened, Jake was at a job site with his dad. Joseph was talking to some of his friends off to the side, where men were using chainsaws to cut up a tree they had taken down to the ground. The men often needed to take large trees down from the land to clear the area so they could build houses. The men stopped their noisy chainsaw machines and called out to Joseph to come over and bring your son, Jake.

He was still chewing on his sandwich when his dad picked him up and carried him to the fallen tree.

Jake had a lot of questions, but none of the answers.

"Hey Joe, show them to little Jake!"

Jake's father was always willing to stop everything if it meant he might be teaching his kids something. It was a nice warm feeling when Jake's dad would show him something new like that.

It made him feel so special. He would look around and be amazed at how all the men were standing there smiling, pointing, and saying things like "Wow, look, Jake," or "Hey Jake, check it out—three baby squirrels in the nest in the tree!"

His father knelt down close to the baby squirrels and picked one up. He held it near his son and would say something like, "Jake, ya see this? One of God's little creations!... So cute and beautiful. What do you think, Jake? God sure had a great idea when He thought of making these beautiful little creatures, don't ya think?"

Jake was amazed at the little animal. It sat in his father's hand like a tiny ball. But it was alive, moving, turning in circles, and rollin' over. His dad held up the baby squirrel to him and said, "See, Jake, see! It's a little baby one, ya see. It's gotta grow up still like you."

"Oh man!" called out one of the construction workers. "Here's one that didn't make it," pointing to the ground near the others.

"Must've gotten thrown when the tree fell."

Joseph walked over a few steps, flicked his cigarette to the ground, and stepped on it to put it out. He looked at the baby squirrel on the ground, which was motionless.

"Poor little guy…"

He never even got a chance to enjoy his life!

The six or seven men stood quietly as Joseph found an empty coffee cup. He removed the plastic lid, scooped the dead squirrel into the cup, and put the lid back on.

"Sometimes these things just happen, Jake," the father explained to his son.

"Maybe that baby squirrel was sick and was going to have a short, sickly life? God knows what's best. He wouldn't want anyone to suffer like that. It's all a part of His plan."

Jake gave a crooked smile, and it was over. The workers began talking again. One of Joseph's foremen brought the three live baby squirrels to the local animal hospital, "so that they could enjoy a good life."

Joseph held onto that coffee cup for the longest time while he finished talking to the workers. He pointed way off to one side of the job and told them how he wanted things to get done.

When Jake got into his dad's pickup truck, he could still see his dad talking. But before long, his dad made his way to the pick-up truck and got in. He set down the coffee cup. Even though Joseph began to talk about something as he started the truck and drove from the job site, Jake half-listened. Curious about the coffee cup and its contents, he would glance over at it now and then. They talked about dinner later and Mom. As Joseph went around a sharp turn, the cup rolled on its side. Joseph set the coffee cup upright again and leaned his book bag against it so it wouldn't fall over again.

When they pulled into the gas station, Jake's mind went off in a different direction. "What had happened to the baby squirrel? Why did God think it was better for him to be in that coffee cup? What was Dad going to do with him next?" Jake had a lot of questions but none of no answers. It made him think a lot. He looked up at the sky and wondered.

"Hey Joseph, what are ya doin' watching the little man today!" the gas station man told Jake's dad.

"Hiya kiddo, fill'er up, what's doin'?" Joseph answered and got out of the truck to walk inside to talk to Tony and Jerry, his mechanic friends. He almost always stopped to talk to them. They were "like family." He knew his dad would be a while when he said, "Be right back, Buddy Boy," it always seemed to take longer when Jake's dad called him Buddy Boy.

Joseph would always make up for it, though, by buying a special treat from the candy machine.

Peanuts, chocolate bars, gum. Jake's dad never came back empty-handed.

The moment that, follows Jake, which he remembers well and thinks about often to this day, in his life as a grown man. Jake moved back his notebook bag and reached for the coffee cup. He held the cup for a little while before he finally moved his thumbs up a bit to pop off the plastic lid.

When he looked into the cup, he saw the dead squirrel. Broken, blood on the bottom of the cup, and motionless. Jake was fascinated by the little creature. When he touched the top of the squirrel's tiny head, he said to himself, "Why did God think it was best if the baby squirrel had died? Why didn't it get a chance to live its life?"

Jake moved his pointer finger on top of the dead squirrel's tiny head a few times. The grey fur moved back and forth with his touch. As he reached closer to the cup, he noticed something different. The fur where he was touching was no longer grey but sort of yellow. It glowed a bit! In the area where he was petting the tiny head, the glow grew from the cup like the flashlight his dad used when he had to work late.

Then suddenly it happened. The tiny squirrel seemed to wake up. It poked its head up and over the rim of the cup, and its two front paws reached for the edge so it could climb out. Within seconds, the tiny squirrel sitting dead in the old coffee cup was climbing onto Jake's shoulder alive and well. The baby squirrel showed no ill effects from the bad tree experience. In fact, the squirrel gave out a chirp as if to say it was happy, playful, and maybe even hungry.

Jake looked up at the sky and whispered, "Thank you!"

"Snickers, M&M's, or dry roasted peanuts, Buddy Boy?" Jake's dad said through the open window as he walked towards the truck with the 3 different treats.

"Let me have the peanuts, Dad."

And he paused a second.

"Squirrels like 'em," Jake answered.

"What's that about squirrels, Buddy B…" Joseph stopped his words as he saw the miracle that had taken place. The dead squirrel was alive and well and climbing playfully on Jake.

"I touched his head and he woke up," Jake told his father. "I'm sorry. Really, Dad, I didn't mean to do anything wrong."

"It's ok." "Ok, really," muttered Joseph as he tried to understand what could have possibly happened.

"Maybe, say… maybe the baby squirrel was just asleep awhile from the tree falling and stuff."

"Huh? Dad," asked Jake.

"Yeah, umm, that must be it," added Joseph.

"That's just great news, Buddy Boy!"

"Come on, let's go home and tell your mother the story. She'd like to hear great news, too," Jake's dad said.

But as he drove off from the gas station after signing the paper, he had a look on his face that Jake had never seen before.

This was the start of it all… and it wouldn't be the last time Jake's dad would have that look.

Chapter 5
So What The "Hell" Happened

Jake, his brother Adam, and his sister Teresa grew up in what could only be described as a wholesome and well-cared-for family environment. Their parents, Joseph and Maria, provided them with stability, values, and a loving home.

They lived in the quiet suburbs of Boston, where the children attended public schools, participated in extracurricular activities, and formed lasting friendships. Sundays were reserved for church, a tradition that reinforced the family's moral foundation. By all outward appearances, they were a typical middle-class family—comfortable, grounded, and actively engaged in the fabric of their community.

Joseph, the father, worked as a foreman for a construction crew. His team was responsible for building both housing developments and small commercial project buildings in the area. Joseph wasn't just a supervisor—he was a craftsman. He had developed his carpentry skills at a young age, having learned them directly from his own father. He later applied and refined these skills on the job, starting as a framer and working his way up.

Through years of dedication and hands-on experience, Joseph earned the respect of his peers. He climbed the ranks by demonstrating natural leadership qualities and excellent interpersonal skills, becoming a figure admired by the 16 men on his crew. His ability to lead wasn't based on authority alone—it was grounded in his work ethic, his fairness, and the way he connected with people.

Maria, Jake's mother, was equally devoted, though in a different way. She was a warm, nurturing presence in the home, especially when the children were young. During those early years, she made the conscious decision to stay home, ensuring that her children received the attention, support, and affection that formed the foundation of their early development.

Once the kids grew older and became more independent, Maria returned to the workforce. She resumed her career in education, taking a position at the local elementary school. Initially, she taught in the lower grades as a classroom teacher, but her passion and aptitude for math eventually led her to a specialized role—assisting students who struggled with the subject. She brought both skill and compassion to her work, just as she had at home.

Adam, Jake's younger brother, was three years his junior. Despite the familial love between them, their relationship was often marked by competition.

From an early age, Adam seemed to be in a constant, unspoken rivalry with Jake. The age gap, rather than bridging their experiences, often widened them. Adam frequently found himself trying to match or exceed Jake's achievements, and this pursuit created tension.

The dynamic between the brothers was further strained by Adam's perception that Jake always came out ahead, whether it was in academics, sports, or parental attention. Even if that belief wasn't always grounded in reality, it was real in Adam's eyes, and that mattered.

As boys, their sibling rivalry sometimes spilled over into physical confrontations—roughhousing that began in play but occasionally took on an edge. School grades became a battleground, as did extracurriculars and approval from their parents. These tensions didn't always come to the surface in obvious ways, but they lingered under the surface. Adam, in particular, harbored a quiet resentment. He constantly felt like he was living in his brother's shadow, always one step behind.

Over time, this sense of being the "lesser" brother began to define how he viewed their relationship. And while Jake may have been unaware of just how deep Adam's frustrations went, they left a lasting mark.

Once school ended, the paths of Jake and Adam diverged more definitively. They went their separate ways, drifting apart not just physically but emotionally. The distance between them grew, and whatever closeness they might have shared as children became more like a memory than a reality. They were no longer the kind of brothers who called each other regularly or leaned on each other for support.

That potential bond—the brotherhood that might have blossomed under different circumstances—never fully developed.

Their younger sister, Teresa, was much younger than both Jake and Adam and as the baby of the family, she was treated accordingly. While Jake and Adam were busy dealing with their own conflicts and challenges, their interactions with Teresa were minimal. Most of their involvement came in the form of typical older sibling duties: helping around the house, watching her perform in school plays, or giving her a ride to soccer practice.

Teresa had her own world, filled with close friendships and a strong bond with their mother, Maria. She spent much of her time alongside Maria, building a different kind of closeness than the boys had with either parent. Her presence in the family completed the picture of a classic American household—full of love, laughter, struggles, and routines. They were, by all accounts, an average family dealing with average problems in an average American neighborhood.

Then everything changed.

What followed was not just a shift, but an upheaval. The details of the war that came next, and the destruction it left behind, are too gruesome and painful to fully recount. The trauma ran deep and touched every part of their lives. The war decimated communities tore families apart, and left lasting scars that words alone cannot capture.

Over the course of three long, devastating years, life as they knew it unraveled. The ordinary world they had once known was replaced by chaos, grief, and survival.

Jake and Adam's parents, Joseph and Maria, and their sister Teresa were among the casualties. They were killed in the war, along with many of their friends, neighbors, and extended family members. The tragedy was staggering. Somehow, Jake and Adam survived—perhaps by chance, perhaps by fate. They had been in the right place at the right time, or at least not in the wrong place. But survival came at a cost.

In the aftermath of the loss, Jake and Adam were left to process their grief alone. Rather than drawing them together, the pain drove them further apart. Each brother coped in his own way. Jake sought meaning in the ruins—he looked for ways to help, to rebuild, to be part of the solution. Adam, on the other hand, struggled to move forward. He remained stuck in the pain, becoming part of the very problems that plagued the world around them.

Time passed—three years—and during that time, the two brothers barely spoke. Their only updates came secondhand, through mutual acquaintances or occasional mentions from distant relatives.

Jake, for his part, carried a quiet ache. Despite everything, he longed for reconciliation. He didn't want their relationship to end in silence or bitterness. In his heart, he hoped to bridge the distance, to resolve whatever unspoken rift had driven them apart. But he didn't know how. He couldn't even identify exactly what had caused the divide. All he could do was guess—that somewhere in the mess of childhood memories, schoolyard rivalries, and years of growing apart, resentment had taken root. And now, it stood like a wall between them.

Chapter 6
Getting To Know You

After returning on the bus to town to catch up on backpack supplies, Jake, Jerry, and Emily walked together along Main St. It was still early morning, but they hoped some stores were open. They each had a list in their pockets of their needs. Just ahead was the Main St. corner, and the garbage collection appeared in full swing.

"Come on, people, it's Friday, time to toss it all away."

Many of the folks looked down at their bags with a sad look on their faces. The lady on the bench got up and threw her bag in the garbage truck.

"Good… good… good. You'll feel a lot better later for doing that."

The lady shuffled away, uncertain, looking down.

"Here we go now, people, it's Friday for cryin' out loud—now's your chance, here's your time to throw away your sins and worries…"

Jake and the others walked on by the busy corner. They all knew what it was about... but didn't comment.

"I wonder if Wally's is open?... They usually have everything," Jerry said.

"I need some personal items," Emily chimed in. "Female stuff."

" Do Dad's?" Jerry chuckled as they walked along toward the stores.

Jake thought it might be a good idea to bring Jerry to his apartment for a shower and a shave and to give him clean, untattered clothing.

"Hey Em, we're gonna swing by my apartment… be back on the avenue in about an hour or so," Jake told her. "Go get your stuff."

"Ok, ok… I'll meet you guys by the spot near the thing where we ate that stuff that time." Emily gave her a unique but typically kooky direction. Jake knew just what she meant, though, as they went their separate ways for now.

Later, they would take the bus back.

The back-and-forth routine continued on for months. Jake, Emily, and Jerry made the trek by bus out to "Renewal Road" and participated in the repairs while they waited around for the next bus of rioters to arrive to inflict property damage. As time went on, they got to know each other, their thoughts, their hopes, their dreams.

Jake wanted someday to be a father, as his father was to him, to teach all the little things he had learned from his dad. The world was different now, though. The fields he used to play on as a child were now piled high with the clean-up debris, which was seemingly ongoing for years. There would be many new lessons to teach one day. It had become a totally different world now than when Jake was young. It was a major concern of his.

Sometimes Jake would wonder if this was even a world to raise children. Many of the changes that had taken place in the past more than three years were oppressive toward the people. The state government had used a heavy hand of control.

He understood why they did what they did… he just enjoyed the way things were before.

Sometimes, the anarchy was something Jake was indeed involved with. But freedom had also been thrown away. Freedom of speech. Freedom of dissent. Even freedom of some thought was punishable by the state.

The state, however, now provided all necessary needs. Food, drinks, and supplies were all free, as long as they fit into your backpack. Travel by bus and train was always available at no cost.

If you needed to see a doctor, treatment and medicine were free, as long as the state deemed it, and you worthy of "repair." Always considered dubious at best.

For this, you had to work to "help" the state. Anything that contributed to an overall positive effect was not just encouraged—it became mandated.

The list of "volunteer" jobs was always posted in federal buildings. The new system seemed to work well enough; however, it did tend to squash out a lot of the character and personality of working in society.

Emily was an attractive woman in her late twenties. Her chestnut hair flowed over her shoulders, and she had a friendly way about her with a lovely smile...

Emily was orphaned at a young age and was essentially on her own from a teenager. She dreamed of what she never had—family, friends, and love. She fit right in with the crew at the Renewal Road job site.

The workers enjoyed Emily's pleasant way. She helped with whatever was needed straightening up, bringing the workers supplies, or even coffee.

Emily was wonderful with all the kids. There were always at least a dozen young girls and boys who sort of watched all the activity from the lake/picnic table areas. They knew not to get too close to the construction site, but they were curious nonetheless. Emily would go over and play games, do art projects, and sing songs with the children. It was always helpful and reassuring to know Emily was there with the kids.

Jerry, on the other hand, was sort of a homeless bum type. He was, in fact, quite ragged, unshaven, and could use a shower. But Jerry was kind. He thought and spoke of others' feelings often. He would share anything he had. and ironically, he never had much. He also would lend a hand every day at the job site, bringing supplies like doors and windows to the workers.

Occasionally, though it wasn't permitted, Emily and Jerry wandered off from the picnic area toward the "riot bus" and briefly spoke to some of the rioters out of curiosity, to try to understand them. As a man came back to the "riot bus," they couldn't help but notice he was carrying the top part of a mailbox.

"Hey, whatcha got there, chief?" Emily asked him.

"Oh, it's a souvenir," the rioter replied.

"Sure, of course, it is," Jerry sarcastically added.

"What do ya hang that on the wall in your office next?"

"To your bowling trophies?"

Emily chuckled silently, then asked,

"Why do you do it?"

"Do what?" His name was Adam.

"Come here to riot and destroy property."

"Why do you like to do that?"

"Oh, I don't know, it's fun, I guess. My friends all come, and it gives you something to do, I guess."

The young rioter wrapped both arms around the mailbox with a hug.

"My sister and parents were killed in the war. It's my way of protesting our society. Our bus is full of our club, 'Fallen Family.' We were all shattered by our old government's decisions, so we protested."

Adam said to tell Jake to fix it all again.

He looked down at his mailbox souvenir and stepped back onto the bus. Emily had a tear in her eye. Jerry saw it, reached out, and gave her a hug.

Others started to walk toward the bus as the destruction was nearly over. Emily and Jerry turned and began walking back to the picnic area… this time holding hands.

Chapter 7
Emily And Jerry

Emily and Jerry walked back towards the picnic area by the lake.

"Do you like me, Jerry?" Emily questioned.

"Sure, of course, I like you, what the heck are you talkin' about?"

"Yes, but do you like me… like me, that's what I'm asking," in her typical kooky way.

They paused their walk back, turned to face each other, embraced, and enjoyed a long, passionate kiss.

"Does that answer your question?" Jerry questioned.

"Yes."

"I gotcha," Emily glowed happily… "You do like me like me!"

They chuckled and continued the walk back.

As they got closer, Jake could see his two friends were now holding hands — he smiled but kept it to himself, thinking they both needed someone and now they've found happiness and it gave Jake a warm feeling on a chilly afternoon.

Emily and Jerry continued to walk back when she asked him another of her questions that often sounded a bit like a riddle.

"Jerry, do you think people fall in love with who they meet or meet who they fall in love with?"

"What?"

"You know what I mean," she jumped back in.

"No, actually I don't," Jerry confirmed.

"I mean, is it just a random act that could happen anywhere to anybody, or is love a part of a master plan directed from a higher power of sorts?"

"Oh, I'm goin' with the higher power theory," Jerry responded.

"So like what?…" Emily pressed on.

"Oh, I don't know," Jerry, now a little frustrated… "maybe it's the sun."

"Hmmm… the sun, interesting, I never thought of that one," Emily finally accepted.

As they got to the picnic table, Jerry ended with…

"Yup — the sun… think about it."

When they got back to the picnic table area, Jake was feeding the stray cats again. The cats all came around every day or so. The kids loved to play with them, and Jake just loved to feed the hungry.

"What were you two doing? You know we're not supposed to talk to the rioters," Jake warned.

"Nothing really, Jake, just a little curious," Emily answered.

"Hey, Jake, this guy said for you to fix it all up again, and he was stealing one of the mailboxes for a souvenir," Jerry chuckled.

"What?" Jake questioned.

"Yeah — this guy Adam…" Emily started.

Jake jumped off the picnic table and started running towards the riot bus.

"What's going on?" Jerry called out.

"Adam's my brother!"

"I'll be back!" Jake hollered.

Chapter 8
Blind Eyes, Clear Purpose

"I've just met a girl named Maria."

Jake sprinted across the cracked asphalt, breath ragged, dust swirling in his wake. The last riot bus was just about to pull away from the park gates when he lunged forward and slapped the side, waving.

With a hiss and a groan, the door creaked open. Behind the wheel sat Nicholas, his old friend, the same lanky guy he ran track with back in high school.

"Hey, what's up, ol' buddy?" Nicholas grinned, voice gravelly with age and road dust. "You sure you're getting on the right bus? This one's full of troublemakers."

Jake, panting slightly, managed a breathless smile and a thumbs-up. "I know, Nick. Just... something important."

Without waiting for a reply, he stepped onto the bus, the scent of sweat, smoke, and adrenaline greeting him like a wall. As Jake walked down the center aisle, the chaotic energy was electric—rowdy cheers, boots stomping, windows fogged from warm breath and tension. For a moment, he flashed back to those track meets—he and Nicholas, neck and neck on the final sprint. That same burning in his lungs flared now.

He scanned the packed seats. Just ahead and to the left, a familiar voice cut through the noise. There, toward the back, was Adam, Jake's younger brother, grinning wildly as he hoisted a bent mailbox triumphantly above his head like a trophy. The crowd around him whooped in approval, fists pounding the seatbacks.

Jake ducked his head, choosing to stay out of the spotlight, and slipped into an empty seat on the right-hand side.

Next to him, a young woman sat quietly by the window, her posture rigid, shoulders slightly hunched inward. Jake slid his backpack down to the floor and cleared his throat gently.

"Hello... I'm Jake."

A pause. Then, softly, "Hello..." she replied, eyes still fixed outside. "Maria," she added. "I mean, my name... It's Maria."

Her voice carried a careful grace, yet a distant sadness. Jake studied her profile—her expression unreadable behind oversized black sunglasses. Something about her seemed... set apart. Detached, even from the chaos surrounding them.

Just then, the bus jolted forward, sending a ripple through the crowd. Laughter erupted in waves. Some hooted, others shouted like they were leaving a championship parade instead of a ruined neighborhood.

As the vehicle rumbled back toward the city, Jake reached into his backpack and pulled out a crinkled bag of pretzels and a bottle of water. He nibbled at one absentmindedly, then turned and held the bag out toward Maria.

"Pretzel?"

She finally turned to face him, slowly, her movements deliberate. Her lips curled into the faintest smile.

"Oh, no, thank you very much," she said, her voice almost a whisper.

Jake noticed the sunglasses again—thick, matte black like the kind beggars on street corners sometimes wore. His heart dipped, a quiet pang surfacing. He remembered those makeshift signs slung across scarred shoulders:

Blind from the war... Please help.

He hesitated, then asked gently, "Do you usually come out to Renewal Road with this group?"

Maria nodded faintly.

"Well, yes," she replied. "My three brothers... they bring me along. It's the club they're members of—'Fallen Families.' We've all lost someone in the war."

Her tone softened, voice lowering as if sharing something sacred.

"That's how I was injured, too. I have a bad limp... and I'm blind."

Jake felt his chest tighten. There was a grace to her honesty, no bitterness, no anger. Just the weight of truth, calmly spoken. She was kind. Gentle. His earlier feeling had been right—she was different.

Suddenly, a young man popped his head over the seat behind Jake. He looked protective, alert.

"Hey, you OK, sis?"

Maria turned slightly toward the voice.

"Yes, we're fine. Just chatting with Jake here."

"Thanks, Peter," Jake said, reaching out to shake the young man's hand. Peter nodded once and disappeared back behind the seat.

For a few minutes, silence fell between them. Jake finished a few more pretzels, took a final sip from his water, and then packed both away. He shifted in his seat, pulled the lever, and reclined.

A gruff voice crackled over the speakers.

"Settle down back there!" Nicholas barked through the old P.A. system.

Jake chuckled to himself. Same Nick. He leaned back, letting the vibrations of the road rock him toward sleep.

And then the memories began to seep in...

The war.

The thunderous blasts that split the sky. The screams. The black smoke. The haunting quiet after.

He saw again the twisted remains of buildings, power lines downed like fallen giants, and the endless scramble for water, for electricity, for survival. Three years ago, society had nearly buckled under the pressure. Chaos ruled. Law was a memory. Gangs roamed freely. Stores were looted. Women were raped. Families vanished overnight. Anarchy had taken the reins.

He had lost so much, his parents. His sister. Friends who felt like family. Names he hadn't spoken to in years because it still hurt too much to say them aloud.

But somewhere inside that grief, something solid had formed. Something resolved.

At age 33, sitting on a battered riot bus next to a blind girl named Maria, Jake Christenson remembered the exact moment he knew:

He had to get involved.

He had to do something.

No matter the cost.

He just had to.

Chapter 9
Dream of the Nightmare

The bus continued its steady rumble toward the city, a low mechanical growl that blended with the occasional loud burst of laughter and shouting coming from the back rows. But none of it was enough to rouse Jake from his much-needed nap. His body remained still, his mind adrift—but far from peaceful. What played out behind his closed eyes wasn't rest, but rather a grim slideshow of memories that returned like an old haunting friend. The dream quickly twisted into a nightmare.

Again, he found himself reliving the horror—the desolation that followed the war. The survivors, hollow-eyed and broken, were struggling not just to find food and shelter, but to grasp even a thread of order in a world that had completely unraveled. Jake had lived those moments once before, but his mind insisted on revisiting them with cruel precision. Endless meetings. Long nights. Agonizing debates. It all played again.

After the collapse, the survivors had cobbled together a semblance of leadership: a "city committee" made up of twelve of the wisest surviving elders—men and women who still carried within them the embers of reason and hope. Their goal was daunting: to restore some framework of civilization before the fragile remnants of society descended into permanent anarchy.

They gathered in the local high school gymnasium, which had become a makeshift town hall. Two to three hundred people crowded inside, seated uncomfortably on cold folding chairs, eyes wide with desperation and suspicion. The air inside was heavy, not just with the heat of tightly packed bodies, but with tension and despair. The meetings often erupted into fierce arguments, harsh language, and even the occasional physical fight. The grief of loss, the fear of tomorrow, and the trauma of survival were not easily tamed.

Despite the chaos, small pockets of progress emerged. Subcommittees were created, given impossible tasks: restoring food distribution, maintaining order, and drafting new social rules. Martial law was implemented almost immediately. Police were placed on military alert twenty-four hours a day, seven days a week. Their presence was unmistakable—grim figures patrolling the streets with automatic, military-grade weapons slung across their chests. The violence did decrease, yes, but so did any remnants of joy. Life became survival. And survival became a gray, joyless routine. Depression and suicide rates quietly climbed behind closed doors.

Eventually, the committee produced an outline—an agreed-upon structure to govern what remained of day-to-day life in the war's aftermath. Radical decisions had to be made. For now, cars have been banned completely. Only buses were allowed in areas where roads remained intact, and trains were used if the rail lines had survived the destruction. These state-controlled forms of transportation were free to use, a small mercy.

So too were food and water, though they came with conditions. Each citizen was issued a standard backpack. Anything they took—be it sustenance or supplies—had to fit inside that pack. Medical care and prescriptions were also free, but only for those considered "repairable" by the state. A chilling word. "Repairable." As though humans were now appliances to be judged worthy of effort or not.

But these "benefits" came with severe trade-offs. Volunteerism was no longer a choice—it was a civic duty. Every physically capable person was required to work for the state in some capacity. And the cost wasn't just labor. Select books were banned, especially those that spoke of religion, independent thinking, or dissent.

Churches, mosques, synagogues, and any house of worship were permanently shut down. Faith had been labeled an obstacle. The new world demanded simplicity, uniformity, and above all, control.

Jake had been an active voice in those meetings, a contributor whose opinions were sometimes even incorporated into policy. But not all of his beliefs were welcome. Many of the more oppressive laws were met with resistance from the people. Protests broke out. Flyers were torn down. But in the end, resistance crumbled. The other side had all the guns.

Jake had been a member of the LTN, the "Love Thy Neighbor" group. Their mission was compassion, grounded in the teachings of the Holy Bible. But their timing was poor. The Theologian Council, now a dominant ruling body, had already banned the Bible. They deemed it a fictional story that had, for centuries, misled the masses and hindered progress. In their official declaration, they ruled that religion existed only because of fear. Remove fear, and you eliminate the need for God.

The council's conclusions were cold and calculated: by eradicating fear, anxiety would lessen. And not just fear—other emotions, too. The Legal Council followed suit with sweeping mandates. Emotions like faith, love, anger, and ambition were now seen not as human traits, but as threats to societal control. In their view, such feelings made people unpredictable and, therefore, dangerous.

Jake had fought hard against these decrees. He stood at the meetings, unwavering, demanding that the basic human rights of the people be preserved. He pleaded, debated, and shouted himself hoarse. But ultimately, the amendment passed. It bore the chilling name: "For the Betterment of Mankind."

And that was that. The new law was the law of the land. Anyone who wished to benefit from the state's offerings had to contribute in some way. Volunteer jobs, everything from public sanitation to military maintenance, were plastered on every telephone pole and inside every building.

Enforcement was visible and aggressive. Armed officers walked the streets at all hours, ensuring compliance and quelling dissent before it had a chance to spread.

Now, Jake found himself in the cruelest position of all. He wasn't just surviving under these new rules—he had become, in part, an enforcer of them. It was a betrayal of his own ideals. A wound that never quite healed.

He remembered clearly the policy surrounding "Riot Roads", an eerie concept that had become normalized. These were designated zones where citizens were legally permitted to engage in acts of controlled violence. The logic was twisted: emotional suppression had failed in the past, notably during the so-called Abstinence Movement. Drugs dulled the pain but created dependency. Emotions couldn't simply be turned off. The answer, then, was to let them out, under supervision.

The state set up specific roads where people could unleash their rage and despair. Scream, fight, destroy. It didn't matter, so long as it stayed within the boundaries of the riot zones. The goal was simple: keep life outside the chaos functioning smoothly.

It was crude but effective. A society stitched together with duct tape and fear.

Jake stirred in his seat.

"Hey... hey guys on the way back, settle down!" Nicholas shouted from the front, trying to bring order to the chaos brewing in the back of the bus.

The rowdy group of teenagers had started tossing Adams' mailbox, yes, an actual mailbox— back and forth like a toy. The noise jolted Jake awake. He blinked rapidly, shaking off the heavy fog of his dream. For a moment, he didn't know where he was. Then his eyes landed on Maria sitting beside him.

This time, he really looked at her. She was calm. Beautiful in a quiet, effortless way. Something about her presence eased the disorientation.

Jake reached into his backpack and pulled out a bottle of water. He took a slow sip just as the bus hissed and screeched to a stop at the station.

The nightmare might have ended, but the world outside hadn't changed.

Chapter 10
Jake And Adam

The brakes of the bus squeaked to a halt. Over the crackling old P.A. system, the driver announced, "Central Station, end of the line for everybody! Nicholas continued... collect all your belongings, backpacks, personal items, and especially any garbage or food. Exit the bus in an orderly manner, and thank you all once again."

Jake stood, slung on his backpack, and offered a sincere goodbye.

"So long. Take care of yourself, Maria... it was so nice to meet you."

"Thank you, Jake... you take care too, you're very kind," Maria replied warmly.

Her brothers were already approaching her seat to help her up. Jake gave each of them, Peter, James, and Jason, a quick fist bump in parting. He remembered the three brothers from high school. Peter had been on the track and cross-country teams. James once starred as the lead in the school play. And Jason... Jason had dreams of becoming a lawyer before everything in society changed. Now, there wasn't much need for lawyers anymore.

Jake stepped off the bus and waited outside. He was expecting a difficult conversation with his brother, Adam, but he was determined to try.

The crowd of rioters outside was still a bit rowdy as they filed off in different directions, some breaking off into small groups.

"Hey!" Jake called out. "Give me that mailbox!" he joked.

"No way, bro! It's my souvenir. What's up anyway?" Adam shot back.

"Not much... I just saw you were with this group, club, whatever you call it. I thought maybe we could sit down somewhere, catch up on stuff... just us two brothers, from the heart." Jake's voice was calm and sincere.

"Okay, okay... I guess you're right. Let's do it," Adam said, relenting. "Let's stop into Wally's... I need some stuff for my backpack."

"Okay, me too," Jake replied, following along.

Inside the store, the brothers picked out supplies, the usual: sandwiches, bottled water, snacks, and a treat or two. Jake also grabbed a box of dry cat food.

Adam glanced over and smirked. "What the hell are ya eatin' that stuff now?"

"No," Jake said, smiling. "I feed the stray cats at Renewal Road. They get hungry too."

"I guess..." Adam muttered, unconvinced.

"All creatures need to eat," Jake added. "The kids are there, and we love them too."

"Okay, okay, I get it. Let's go," Adam said, heading for the door. "Thanks, Walley!" he called out with a thumbs-up as he left the store.

Jake followed just behind and gave Walley a friendly wave. As he stepped outside, his thoughts lingered.

It might be really tough getting through to Adam, he thought, and I just hope he hasn't gotten too radicalized.

Outside again, Adam took the lead, pointing in the direction of his apartment.

"Let's go."

"How far?" Jake asked.

"Just five or six blocks," Adam assured him.

"Hey, little brother, it's only like three or four blocks to a major condemned area. Still isolated from the damage caused by the bombings," Jake warned, his tone cautious.

"Don't worry, don't worry... It's all good," Adam replied sarcastically, playing the role of big brother with a smirk.

They continued on, turning off Main Street and heading down 8th Avenue, blatantly ignoring the Do Not Enter signs. Two blocks in, they turned onto Cherry Lane. Now the destruction was impossible to ignore, not just around them, but beneath their feet. Rubble was scattered in every direction, a chaotic mosaic of crumbled concrete, twisted metal, and shattered glass.

These neighborhoods had never been cleared. Demolished buildings and debris still cluttered the streets. The city simply didn't have enough manpower or equipment to clear block after block of bombed-out ruins.

Adam and Jake carefully stepped over the uneven terrain, navigating the wreckage with raised knees and cautious footing.

"Toto, I've got a feeling we're not in Kansas anymore," Jake muttered, half to himself.

"What? What the hell are you talkin' about?" Adam snapped.

"Oh... It's one of Dad's old jokes. Never mind, for now," Jake replied, letting the moment pass.

"OK, it's in here." Adam veered toward a worn-out brownstone building. The exterior had taken some hits but stood mostly intact. Even so, Jake immediately had doubts. If this was Adam's idea of a good place to live, maybe he had gone too far... maybe he was radicalized, and his judgment, compromised.

They entered the building and climbed two narrow, creaking flights of stairs to reach Adam's apartment. When they reached the door, Adam swung it open and stepped aside.

"So... what do ya think?" he asked, motioning Jake inside.

Jake stepped through the doorway and paused. He didn't want to be harsh, but he also didn't want to lie. He needed to be honest... carefully.

The walls were a dark grey. The ceiling was too. There was a couch and two chairs, with nothing on the walls except a family photo, taken maybe twelve to fifteen years ago. A small kitchen area held a table and three mismatched chairs. Off to the side was a bathroom, and straight ahead, a bedroom.

The place said a lot about Adam's state of mind. Jake could feel it, the heaviness. Adam must be very depressed.

"Hey Adam, if it meets your needs, and you're comfortable, and you like it, well then, it's okay by me," Jake said, lying just to break the silence and start a conversation.

Adam sat down in one of the sofa chairs near the couch. His shoulders slumped, and after a moment, he began to cry.

"I can't seem to get out of this funk I've been in. I thought this dark hole feeling would pass, but sometimes everything just seems hopeless. I've even considered ending it all... but I figured I'd screw that up too," Adam confessed between sobs.

"Why do ya stay here alone, in this dark and dreary place?" Jake asked, his voice soft.

"Because this is how I feel!" Adam shouted back, his sorrow now tangled with anger. "Nobody cares about me. Nobody ever cared about me. Why should I care about myself?"

The words hit the room like a wave, full of pain, frustration, and years of silence. Adam wasn't just yelling at Jake; he was yelling at the past, at the memories, at the emptiness.

Adam Christenson was now twenty-nine years old, about three and a half years younger than Jake. And that age gap, though small, had always felt like a mountain Adam couldn't climb.

To him, it was more than just sibling rivalry. It wasn't just about sports, school grades, or even friendships and dating. It ran deeper. Adam had always felt different somehow... less, even from his own parents.

He could never fully explain it, but the feeling was constant. The belief that Jake got special attention. That Jake was the favorite.

For as far back as Adam could remember, there were always those little reminders, always for Jake.

"Be careful, Jake... remember what we told you!"

Or:

"Don't worry if you don't get it done today, Jake... tomorrow's another day."

And somehow, tomorrow was always today, but never for Adam.

"Yesterday, anyway, things can always change."

Why did Jake always seem to get special attention?

Adam felt the time had come to bring it all up to clear the air and settle their differences once and for all. And so, the two brothers finally talked it out. Right there in that dark, dingy room with its worn, dirty furniture and a dented mailbox sitting oddly on the kitchen table.

Their conversation stretched on for quite a while. Adam raised his voice more than once, desperate to make his points heard. And though Jake did his best to explain, to be gentle, to offer reasons, much of it, to Adam, felt hollow... like something was still being withheld.

"What the hell are you not telling me? Dammit, I *deserve* to know the truth!" Adam shouted, his voice shaking with frustration.

Jake hesitated, thinking. Then, a memory. Another old movie quote surfaced in his mind.

"YOU CAN'T HANDLE THE TRUTH!"
—*A Few Good Men.*

The line echoed in Jake's thoughts. He paused. Slowly, he looked around the room again, that same heaviness returning. His gaze landed on the dented mailbox. Then on Adam. Finally, he stood.

"Okay," Jake said. "Here goes... let me show you something. Something I promised Mom and Dad I'd keep secret."

Without another word, Jake walked over to the old, stained couch. He reached out and touched it with his right hand.

And then... everything changed.

Suddenly, a hologram filled the room. It shimmered to life like a memory returning in vivid light. There they were their **Mom and Dad**, and their little sister **Teresa**, playing with Barbie dolls on the coffee table. The atmosphere was warm, safe, and surreal.

A younger Jake, maybe twelve years old, stepped into the projection. His voice, small and high-pitched, echoed in the room.

`"Adam doesn't want to watch the movie. He'd rather play with his army men in his room."`

Adam, stunned, jolted back. His eyes darted from the hologram to Jake.

"What the hell is this?" he shouted.

"How are you doing this?"

"That's our old house on Mohawk Ave."

"What's going on here, Jake!" Adam demanded.

"Just be patient and watch," Jake recommended.

Back to the hologram...

`"Joseph, I'll make the popcorn,"` *Maria said.*

`"OK, honey."`

"Dad, what's the name of the movie we're watching tonight?" young Jake questioned.

"It's Casablanca. It takes place during World War II. It has everything... patriotism, heroism, and a love story."

"Joseph, the garbage can is full and needs to go out," Maria called from the kitchen.

Joseph hollered back, "Frankly, my dear... I don't give a damn."

Jake and his dad laughed out loud.

"That was a line from last week's movie Gone with the Wind."

They watched dozens of movies together back then in that family room on Mohawk Ave. It was something they always enjoyed together, something, for some reason, Adam just didn't seem to have the patience for.

"Ooh, hot buttered popcorn!" their mom, Maria, said in a sing-song voice. "And Joseph, don't talk fresh like that in front of the kids."

"That was a line from a movie."

"I don't care... it wasn't funny and it was disrespectful."

"OK — OK... the movie's about to start..."

"Can I have popcorn, Mom?" Teresa called out.

"Sure, sweetie, here you go. See if Barbie wants some too."

"This is killing me, Jake. Why and how are you showing me old home movies?" Adam shouted in protest.

"Be patient... here it comes," Jake assured.

"OK, tell him what we've both decided," Maria told Joseph.

"OK, yes... Jake, your mom, and I discussed this in great detail, and we would like for you to keep your 'special gift' a secret. That means under no circumstance do you tell anyone about it. None of your friends, or those at school, or even your brother and sister. This 'special gift' is to remain a total secret. Perhaps someday, when you're older, you will have the correct judgment to decide how and when to properly use this 'special gift.' There will be no further discussion on it. Please don't disappoint us."

"I won't, Dad and Mom. I promise."

"OK... here comes the movie..."

"Got any more popcorn?" Joseph called out.

Then the hologram disappeared.

"And so what's that supposed to mean, anyway?"

Adam, angry and unconvinced, shouted at Jake.

"What kind of trick was that?"

"That was no trick. That's what happened that day in our old family room at our old house," Jake sincerely assured.

"Come on, cut it out... don't pull my leg. It was some sort of trick."

"And what was this all about, a 'special gift'?" Adam asked.

"That is why I showed you that. To tell you that I, your brother Jake, was born, I guess with a gift or ability or power to do things like what you just saw... and much more."

"OK, Jake, OK. I get it. I don't want to argue anymore. Do ya know how to get back to the bus stop?"

"Sure."

"I'm goin' in there and gonna crash out, 'cause I'm dead tired. Just let yourself out, and maybe I'll see you around sometime. Maybe when our club comes out to bang up Renewal Road," Adam chuckled and went into his bedroom.

"OK, little brother," Jake called out. "Hope to see ya soon."

At one point Adam went into the other room and came out with a cardboard box. He put it on the kitchen table and just said,

"Here Jake, you can take stuff with you when you go."

Inside the box were family pictures, framed and unframed along with Christmas string lights and ornaments, and assorted small trinkets from shelves and cupboards of their parents' old house. Sticking out was their dad's old guitar that he used to play often.

"Just take it, Jake… I don't want to look at it any longer."

Jake silently nodded that he would take it when he left.

Jake picked up his backpack, put it over his shoulders, and took the steps toward the door to leave. He paused at the exit of the apartment, then touched the wall next to the door and instantly turned the walls and ceiling bright yellow. Then he walked out.

Chapter 11
The End Of The Beginning

Jake walked out of Adam's apartment carrying a deep, melancholy sadness and disappointment. He hadn't been able to resolve the differences with his brother. Still, he felt he had given it a sincere effort and held onto hope that someday—perhaps sooner rather than later—they might find a way to make things right.

He descended the creaky, worn stairway and stepped out into the devastated, war-torn neighborhood. Carefully, he made his way through chunks of concrete, damaged wood, and scattered shards of broken glass. As he slowly headed toward the bus terminal, his thoughts drifted back over the recent events—how Jerry and Emily seemed to have sparked a loving relationship, how he had abruptly left Renewal Road and hoped his work crew had the repairs under control, and of course, blind young Maria… and Adam.

As he neared the corner—

He could already hear the loud garbage truck hissing and grinding in the distance. It was garbage day again. The tall, skinny man with the wooden board was out there doing his usual routine, delivering his impassioned sales pitch to those still unsure whether it was time to confess their sins and toss them away. Jake recognized Axel from his old neighborhood. His mother and Axel's had once been good friends, they used to swap recipes, play cards with others, and go to the mall together.

Those memories felt like they belonged to another lifetime. Jake wondered how his family had even made it through the war.

"Okay, people, it's Friday… time to get rid of it once and for all and start with a clean slate!" Axel shouted.

As Jake reached the corner, he waved to Chris, who was up in the cab of the garbage truck, driving today. Chris gave him a thumbs-up, which Jake returned to both men.

"Let's go, people! We won't be back till Wednesday, so get rid of it now—believe me, you'll feel better for it!"

Jake glanced up and saw that the next bus heading to Renewal Road was due to arrive any minute. He found a bench, took a few deep breaths, and waited.

Soon enough, he boarded the bus for the long ride back to rejoin his construction crew and friends at Renewal Road.

When he finally arrived, he noticed a group gathered by the lake and picnic table area. Jogging over, he could already hear the laughter of children as Jerry performed tricks using random objects from his backpack. Nearby, three boys were skipping stones across the lake—one, two, three, four…

"Now you try to top that, Charlie!" little Luca shouted.

Jake joined the group, jumping right into the conversation.

"Hey, what's up, gang?"

Emily, Jerry, Marcus, and Jonathan were all sitting at the same table.

"Where ya been, Jake?" Marcus asked.

"Oh, please… don't ask. I'll tell you all later. Just a rough day."

The kids came over, each giving Jake a high five.

"This is what I missed today… a bunch of happy faces and high-fives!" Jake said with a laugh.

Jerry paused a game of tic-tac-toe he was playing with Salena and looked over.

"Jake, what the heck do these folks get out of damaging property anyway? And why does it feel like there's an endless supply of rioters coming after Renewal Road?"

Jake shrugged and replied,

"Who knows… I guess a lot of these rioters are still carrying heavy grief from the war. They've got pent-up anger, and for some, violence just becomes an instinctive release."

Jerry looked up at the bright sky and said, "Today was tomorrow yesterday… It's sad so many folks can't enjoy their lives on beautiful days like this—with the sun and everything."

Jake nodded in agreement, stood up, gave Jerry a friendly slap on the back, and started heading back to the job site.

"Marcus and Jonathan, come take a walk with me!" Jake called out.

"Hey, Jake" Emily chimed in, "All work and no play… you know what I mean. An apple a day—oh gosh… I used to think I was indecisive, but now I'm not so sure!"

It was typical of Emily, offering her usual kooky advice. Jake looked back, shook his head with a smile, then continued on.

The reconstruction had been completed once again, and the entire crew made their way over to the bakery store. It was the only building out of the six along Renewal Road that had working heat, plus tables and chairs inside. By the time it reached four or maybe four-thirty, the air outside had turned noticeably cooler. The crew always referred to the bakery as the "Fake Bake," but in truth, it served as a great shelter whenever the weather took a turn.

There were six large tables inside with plenty of chairs, and park benches lined the perimeter walls. Behind the counter was a storage area, originally meant for bakery goods, but now repurposed.

Jake and his crew used it to stash their backpacks and personal items. Jake had placed the box he brought back from Adam there for safekeeping—family photos, little knick-knacks, his dad's guitar, and even some old Christmas decorations. It felt like the right place for them, out of sight and out of mind, at least for now.

More people were filing into the "Fake Bake" now, shaking off the fresh snow as they entered.

"That must have just started," someone said.

"Coming down pretty good out there," Jonathan observed.

"Yeah, it's starting to stick and pile up!" Matt added.

"I doubt it's gonna amount to anything much," Thomas offered his opinion.

The construction crew's table was lively, conversations picking up as the snow thickened outside.

Jerry and Emily were seated at a separate table with the kids. Jerry was in the middle of a tic-tac-toe match with little Billy. Emily had Liza, Lana, and Salena singing "Jingle Bells," trying to keep the atmosphere cheerful.

Just then, the door opened again. Jake entered, covered in snow, shaking most of it off near the entrance.

"Hey, Jake!" Luca greeted him.

"Come on in and get warm."

"Join us over here, Jake," Marcus called out, inviting their crew supervisor to the table.

The room buzzed with warm conversation, bursts of singing, and festive excitement. The mood was high, sprinkled with laughter, high-fives, and back slaps.

It was rare indeed to feel joy return so fully.

Emily got up from her table and made her way to the computer behind the counter. She searched online for a song that might help carry the festive spirit a little further. Reading aloud from the screen, she said:

"This one might do the trick!" she shouted to Jerry and the girls at the table.

She printed out several copies and handed three or four to each table.

Then, climbing onto her chair in her always-kooky fashion, she made an announcement.

"This is an old song people used to sing over a hundred years ago to cheer themselves up… during a time called the Great Depression. I mean, seriously, what was so great about it?"

Jerry smirked and replied, "No… oh forget it, I'll tell ya later. Let me see the lyrics and music."

Jerry, who played the guitar well and could sing too, got ready to lift the room even higher.

Jake stepped behind the counter and pulled out the box he had gotten from Adam. From it, he carefully took out his dad's old guitar and handed it to Jerry. As Jerry began to tune the instrument, the kids gathered eagerly around him and Emily.

Jerry strummed a few chords, adjusting the strings until the sound was just right. Emily beamed with excitement—she had made this little concert happen.

"It's depressionish, I guess," Emily giggled.

"It's kind of… sorta sorta," Jerry said with a grin.

"Okay, let's try it," Jerry announced.

The Best Things in Life Are Free

The moon belongs to everyone—

The best things in life are free

The stars belong to everyone

They gleam there for you and me

The flowers in spring—the robins that sing

The sunbeams that shine

They're yours—they're mine!

And love can come to everyone—

The best things in life are free.

"Let's try it again!" Emily shouted.

"This time, everybody sings louder…"

As the group began singing once more, Jake quietly reached back into Adam's box and pulled out an old Christmas ornament. He held it in his hand for a long moment, remembering how he used to hang it on the tree as a kid. It felt like a lifetime ago, those days with Adam, Teresa, Mom, and Dad, decorating the tree together inside and out for Christmas.

He wiped a tear from his eye, grabbed his coat, and stepped outside into the snowy night.

A fresh layer of snow, two or three inches, now covered the ground. Jake looked down the stretch of Renewal Road at the six buildings:

The barbershop.

The bakery.

The convenience store.

(All of them "fake.")

Then came the three houses, all of them glowing in the night. All repaired. All shining again.

Even the small details were intact: signs in the windows, and a schedule posted in the barbershop window for a high school basketball team that didn't really exist.

All the details were there and ready.

All except one.

Jake reached into his top pocket and pulled out the Christmas ornament. He held it for a moment, then said aloud with a grin, "Why not!"

From the bakery, he could still hear the cheerful voices singing The Best Things in Life...

Jake gently rubbed his pointer finger across the surface of the ornament, then reached out and touched the corner of the barbershop building.

In an instant, everything transformed.

The entire block became a shimmering Christmas village. Lights sparkled on every corner of all six buildings, casting a warm, colorful glow. Inflated characters stood proudly, Santa Claus, reindeer, snowmen, and even a nativity scene.

It was beautiful. Just as Jake had remembered it could be. Every little detail had been brought to life. Wreaths were hung on each door and window, and a towering Christmas tree stood perfectly decorated in the center of the village square. Even mistletoe was strung above each doorway.

Jake estimated there had to be over three thousand Christmas lights stretched across the buildings. He could still hear the singing echoing from inside the bakery when he spotted a pair of headlights in the distance—glowing through the snow.

It was a bus.

He listened to the muffled crunch of its tires rolling across snow-covered Renewal Road as it finally came to a stop in front of the stores. Jake approached the door, and Nicholas, the bus driver, opened it with a sheepish smile.

"Jake, sorry, man. We got stuck in a snowbank a ways back!"

"I'll say," Jake replied. "You're at least three hours late."

"I know. Didn't want to turn back, so here we are," Nicholas said.

"Alright, listen up," Jake said firmly. "No rioting. Not tonight. How many you got in there?"

"Thirty-six," Nicholas replied. "And yeah, they were pretty rowdy on the way."

He looked around, taking in the lights.

"The place looks beautiful… too bad they want to bust it all up," Nicholas finished.

"Do I hear singing, Jake?" he added.

"Yup. Not a good night for destruction," Jake said.

Just then, a few passengers began stepping off the bus.

"Hold on there, rioters," Nicholas called out. "I'm still talking to the supervisor."

"Hey… real good packing snow, guys!" one of the usual rioters called back to the others still inside the bus.

Some folks from the bakery had started to wander outside into the snowy night. Everyone stood in awe, marveling at the transformation, the lights, the wreaths, the festive wonder of it all.

Children burst out laughing and started playing in the snow. It didn't take long before someone packed together a snowball and let it fly.

Moments later, laughter rang out as a full-on snowball fight broke out, kids, parents, and Jake's work crew versus a busload of Renewal rioters.

The snowballs flew back and forth, laughter echoing through the snowy night. No one was getting hurt, just good old-fashioned fun with joyful shouts and the kind of energy that reminded everyone what peace could feel like.

Jake stepped back inside to warm up and made his way over to the table where Jerry and Emily were sitting, reaching into the old box of family keepsakes, Jake pulled out a familiar pair of his dad's sunglasses.

"Jerry, here ya go, buddy. These were my dad's. I want you to have them," Jake said. "I know how you're always looking up and talking about the bright sun."

A blank expression settled on Jerry's face as he carefully accepted the glasses.

"Thanks, Jake. I mean, your dad's sunglasses and all…" He paused, then looked Jake in the eye.

"But I gotta correct you, my friend. When I talk about the sun, I'm not referring to the bright, hot one in the sky. It's always been my way of referencing the Son of God."

Jake's eyes widened.

"Oh, man. Wow. Now I get it. I wondered a few times, but yeah… The Son of God. Wow," he said, shaking his head in awe.

"A blessed reminder for sure."

Emily and Jerry embraced, sharing a kiss over the touching moment.

Just then, the door of the "Fake Bake" swung open again, letting in a gust of winter air and the sound of the ongoing snowball fight outside, in stepped Adam, Jake's brother.

"Hey! You really spruced up the neighborhood, big brother!" he called out with a grin.

Jake rose from his seat and the two shared a long, emotional bro hug. Jake's heart was lighter than it had been in years.

"If I knew you were coming, I'd have gotten you something special," Jake said with a grin.

"Oh, that's okay. My bright yellow apartment was just fine," Adam laughed.

They sat at a table and talked for a long while, catching up on old times, family memories, friends, and Christmases past and present. And now, even a more hopeful future.

All around them, there was laughter, singing, and a snowball fight. Not a riot. For once, peace had come to Renewal Road.

Chapter 12
The Beginning of The End

Jake leaned in toward his brother and asked quietly, "Did your whole club show up today?"

Adam chuckled, the lines at the corners of his eyes crinkling with warmth. "Yup, they're all out there right now, having a snowball fight with your workers and the kids. It's a madhouse."

Jake grinned but his gaze wandered toward the front windows of the bakery, eyes narrowing slightly as if searching for something or someone.

"Excuse me for a minute… I gotta check on something," he said, already halfway up from the table.

Before stepping away, Jake paused and turned back. "Jerry, Emily, this is my brother, Adam."

Emily squinted, then snapped her fingers. "Oh yeah! You're the mailbox guy!" she said with a laugh. "So… what did you ever do with it?"

Jake didn't answer. He simply smiled, gave a light nod, and slipped out the front door, the bakery bell jingling softly behind him.

Outside, snowflakes drifted down like soft feathers from the heavens, blanketing the world in white. Jake walked briskly, boots crunching against the fresh powder. He passed the organized chaos of laughter and flying snow, his construction crew dodging snowballs like children, some of the actual children singing in off-key, joyous tones:

"Jingle bells, jingle bells, jingle all the way…"

He waved quickly, offering a few smiles, but didn't slow. His focus lay beyond the play and music, at the old bus parked near the edge of the lot, its windows glowing dimly in the snow-dusted night.

As he approached, the bus door creaked open and Nicholas stuck his head out, grinning.

"Hey, what's up, old buddy!" Nick said, his usual infectious enthusiasm brightening the chilly air.

"Hiya, Nick," Jake returned warmly. "Is Maria back there?"

"Yeah, sure, she's in the back."

Jake nodded and stepped inside. The warm, dusty air of the bus hit him instantly. He made his way down the narrow aisle, the overhead lights flickering faintly as the heater hummed below. About ten or twelve rows back, he spotted her, Maria, sitting quietly, hands folded in her lap, her blind gaze turned slightly toward the window as if she could sense the world outside.

He hesitated a moment, then let his heart take over.

"Hi Maria… it's Jake," he said gently, voice soft, respectful.

Her head turned. "Oh yes… hello, Jake," she replied, a small smile on her lips.

"I just wanted to sit and talk a bit, if that's okay?"

"Of course," she said, gesturing to the empty seat beside her. "Have a seat, Jake."

He sat down, brushing snow off his jacket. "You cold? Need anything?" he asked.

"No, I'm fine. Thank you."

Jake smiled, then added with a touch of nostalgia, "You know… my mother's name was Maria, too."

There was a pause, a small space where the past and present hung between them.

Jake had been deeply curious about her ever since their first meeting. There was something about Maria, something more than the obvious. He'd sensed it in her calm, her guarded demeanor, the quiet dignity with which she carried her blindness. He understood now—she was protecting herself. People often saw her condition before they saw her.

Maria asked, "How are things out there? What's happening?"

Jake leaned back, letting his words paint a picture. "It's beautiful, Maria. Snow everywhere. Lights glowing on every building. Kids singing carols and throwing snowballs at my workers… and winning."

Maria let out a breathy laugh, her face lighting up. "I love snow! It sounds fantastic. So much fun… I just wish I could enjoy it more."

Jake looked at her for a long moment, then spoke without hesitation. "You can."

Her brow furrowed. "How? What do you mean?"

He reached slowly toward her hand, resting gently near her side. "Maria… may I touch your face? With my fingers, I mean. I promise I'd never hurt you."

She hesitated. He saw it, the flicker of fear, of disbelief. But then she nodded, voice trembling slightly. "Sure, Jake."

With the utmost tenderness, Jake reached forward and ran his fingers across her forehead, then down, tracing the outline of her closed eyelids. His hands were warm, reverent. And then… the glow.

He could feel it like he always did. That strange, familiar sensation surged beneath his fingertips.

"Open your eyes, Maria," he whispered.

She did, and for the first time in years, or maybe ever, she saw.

She gasped, a sound somewhere between a sob and a laugh, and covered her mouth with both hands. "Jake… I—I can see you…"

From the front of the bus, Nicholas shouted, "Everything okay back there, guys?"

"Yup, we're good, Nick!" Jake replied.

"Yes… yes, we're fine," Maria added, almost giggling with delight.

She turned to him, eyes wide. "How did you do this? Jake… how?"

Jake shrugged, still trying to catch his breath. "I don't know. I really don't. Ever since I was a kid, I've had this… ability. I don't know if it's a blessing or a curse."

Maria reached out and touched his arm. "A curse? No… it's not that."

Jake sighed, looking away. "Maybe. But I can't tell anyone. I'd be the freak of the month."

She shook her head. "I'm not so sure. You could do a lot of good with your talents."

Then, without warning, Maria leaned in and kissed him, deeply, fully. A kiss that spoke of gratitude, longing, and the spark of something new. Jake felt warmth rush through him, an emotion he hadn't felt in years.

Then he pulled back slightly and asked, "Which leg?"

Maria tapped her right leg.

Jake lowered his hand and placed it gently on her thigh. There was another surge of energy, stronger this time. A visible shiver passed through Maria.

"Stand up," he said.

Cautiously, she did. She stood, strong, balanced, whole.

Tears welled in her eyes. "What am I going to tell my brothers? My friends? How will I explain this?"

Jake offered a gentle smile. "Let's go for a walk in the snow. We'll talk it over. See what we come up with."

Maria laughed, a bright sound like wind chimes. "Okay, sounds great."

They bundled up in coats, hats, and gloves, and made their way toward the front of the bus.

"Have fun, you two!" Nicholas called. "Be careful, it's slippery. She's okay, right, Jake?"

"All good. Thanks, Nick," Jake said, shaking his hand. "And have a Merry Christmas too."

"You too!" Nick replied.

Outside, the snow had picked up again, shimmering in the warm glow of the Christmas lights. Instead of turning left toward the noise and chaos of the snowball fight, Jake and Maria turned right, down Renewal Road.

"It's beautiful," Maria whispered. "Jake… all the lights, the snow, the feeling, it's just magical. I feel like we're walking through Munchkinland from The Wizard of Oz."

They strolled past the six buildings that made up Renewal Road, their steps slow, intentional. Along the way, they talked, truly talked.

They asked about each other's families, childhoods, dreams, and losses. To their surprise, they had more in common than either could've guessed. Same schools, and similar upbringings. Jake was six years older, which explained how they'd never crossed paths before.

But Maria had known his sister, Teresa. Hearing that Teresa, along with Jake's parents, had died in the war brought a solemn silence.

Maria shared her own losses. The war had taken pieces of her too. In some strange, poetic way, it was that same war, so cruel and senseless, that had now brought them together.

They stopped for a moment. Snowflakes dusted their shoulders like stars fallen from the sky.

"There's no place like home," Maria said softly.

Jake smiled. "Another Wizard of Oz reference?"

"Did you guys watch a lot of old movies growing up?" she asked.

"All the time," Jake said. "We had whole scripts memorized."

Maria laughed. "Oh my God, us too. We could recite whole scenes."

At the end of Renewal Road, they turned around and started walking back toward the laughter and music.

"So… do you like popcorn?" Jake asked with a grin. "And kids?"

"Yes, yes. Of course! Buttered, please!"

"The popcorn or the kids?" he teased.

They both burst into laughter, genuine, rolling, tear-inducing laughter.

Neither had laughed like that in years. Jake paused. "Are you getting cold?"

"A little."

They turned to face each other again, snow falling around them like confetti in a private celebration. Jake pulled her close, and they kissed again, deep and real.

Suddenly, a snowball whizzed by and smacked Jake in the back. They both yelped, then laughed even harder. Jake bent down, packed a snowball, and held it aloft.

Then, with a gleam in his eye and a smile full of memories, he looked at Maria and said in his best Humphrey Bogart impression:

"Maria… I think this is the beginning of a beautiful friendship."

Maria beamed. "Yes, I think you're right."

And together, hand in hand, they joined the snowball fight, their laughter echoing down Renewal Road, where joy, second chances, and love had finally found their way home.

THE END

www.ingramcontent.com/pod-product-compliance
Lightning Source LLC
Chambersburg PA
CBHW060613310726

48982CB00003B/542